The Veterinarian's Sweetheart

Cheryl Wright

Contents

The Veterinarians Sweetheart

Book 2

Callahan Brothers Series

Copyright 2017 by Cheryl Wright

From the Author

He's been gone more than 18 years now, but I'll never forget the rodeos my dad (and mother) took us to as kids. We looked forward to going each and every year.

Born in the country (as we kids were), my dad was a country man through and through. His first ever job was at a rodeo. He went on to become a ranger, and a horse breaker, amongst other things. His brother looked after horses all his working life, including taking tourists on trail rides. Every now and then I managed to insinuate myself into those trips.

I grew up with horses and the country ways of doing things. And I'm so glad I did.

Sadly, we moved to the city down the track, but I loved (and still love) horses so much, I spent nearly all my extra money and most of my weekends going on horse rides.

Thanks

Thanks to my very dear friends (and authors), Margaret Tanner and Susan Horsnell.

Without their encouragement, this book would not be written.

Thanks also to Alan, my husband of 42 years, who has been a relentless supporter of my writing for many years.

Chapter One

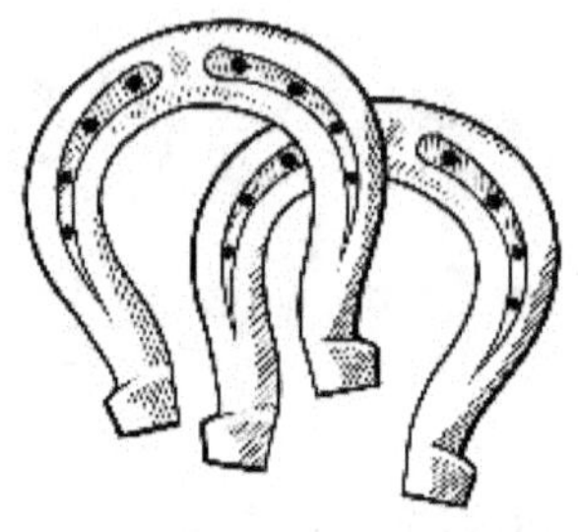

It had been a long night.

Jordon Callahan had been called to a help deliver a foal. Normally it would be a simple task, and the ranch owner would handle it himself.

But the foal was a breach, and that complicated things.

At one stage it looked like they might lose the foal, or the mare, or both. He was determined it wouldn't happen on his watch. As she lay on the hay in her stall, the mare kicked frantically, tossing her head from side to side, making strained noises.

He'd managed to keep her calm early on, but as the hours rolled on, and it got into the early hours of the morning, Jordon knew he was going to have to intervene.

He rolled up his sleeves, donned his long rubber gloves and reached inside the mare, feeling for the foal's legs. She heaved and kicked at his intrusion, but he finally found the tiny legs, and tugged with all his might.

He slowly but surely pulled the foal out of its mother, then gently laid him on the hay. With the rancher and his wife looking on, they all watched and waited for him to get to his feet. But he didn't.

Jordon grabbed a towel and began to rub the foal vigorously, hoping to get it moving. He stood the foal, watching for it to support itself.

They all breathed a sigh of relief when the young foal gingerly stood alone. His exhausted mother nudged him with her head, and began to lick him clean from where she lay on the hay.

He sat with mother and foal for the next hour, to ensure the foal was out of danger, sipping coffee offered by the rancher's wife. He'd need it to drive home safely.

"Thanks Jordon," the rancher said as he was leaving. "I don't know what would have happened if you hadn't intervened." He shook Jordon's hand vigorously, ensuring the vet understood how truly grateful he was.

* * *

Grace Black had no idea what she was going to do.

Out in the middle of nowhere, pulling a horse trailer behind her – complete with horse – and now she was stuck in a ditch.

She was doing perfectly fine until she took that last turn. She must have closed her eyes only momentarily, but it was enough to send her off the road.

She should have stayed in the motel she passed a few hours back, but didn't want to leave her horse alone outside. Besides, she was determined to reach her destination by early morning.

She hadn't seen her best friend Missy Callahan for many months, long before Missy's wedding. She was so bummed she couldn't go to the wedding, but she was on the circuit, and needed to stay the course until it finished for the season. Missy was sad, but totally understood.

Now the grueling season had ended, Grace decided to surprise her friend. She packed up some clothes, loaded her horse Spirit into the horse trailer, and headed for River Valley Montana.

But now here she was. Truck in the ditch, trailer balancing precariously, and no cell reception.

She was so exhausted after the long hours of driving that she couldn't think straight.

She straightened her shoulders and took a deep breath.

First things first. Get Spirit out of that trailer in case it rolled. That would be heartbreaking, to say the least.

As she reached for the reins, she heard a sound. Not just any sound, but an engine. She breathed a sigh of relief and then began to shake.

Hopefully this motorist could help her out of her predicament. As he rounded the corner he slowed and looked her way. He stared at her truck down in the ditch. Then came to a sudden stop.

"You alright?" He looked as tired as she felt.

She stared him down. *Did he really ask her that?*

"Sorry, of course you're not alright. Your truck is down a ditch." He rubbed his fingers across his stubbled chin, and brushed his straggly blonde hair out of his eyes. "I've been up all night," he offered. "Obviously not thinking straight." He smiled at her, and his whole appearance changed.

She held tight onto Spirit's reins in case he was startled by this stranger. "Thanks, I could really do with some help," she said, walking toward the stranger, her horse trailing behind her.

He extended his hand to her. "Jordon Callahan, local vet," he said. She savored his big warm hand. Felt safer with him around. She was beginning to get spooked out here alone in the wilderness.

She shook herself. "Callahan? Any relationship to Missy Callahan?" she asked, flabbergasted at this total and utter coincidence.

He chuckled, his eyes opened wide now. "Brother in law. Missy is married to my brother." He then looked wary. "How do you know Missy?"

She was taken aback. Suddenly he was giving *her* the inquisition? She held tighter onto Spirit's reins, wondering if she was doing the right thing telling this stranger anything.

Of course you are! He's Rory's brother. She shook herself again.

"Missy and I are friends," she said. "We worked together at the rodeo." She rubbed her hands down her jeans clad legs. "For a long time," she added, as though that explained everything.

He stepped toward her slowly, then leaned down to Spirit's legs. "Making sure he's okay," Jordon told her quietly. "In case he was injured in the accident."

Her heart softened. Jordon was kind. He was being kind to her, and to her beautiful Chestnut. She was sure everything would be alright.

* * *

Jordon's call to Rory, Missy's husband, had a band of helpers driving out in the middle of the night, to the middle of nowhere to rescue her and Spirit.

Her heart thumped in her chest as she saw headlights rounding the corner. The very same corner she had miscalculated.

As the truck slowed, the passenger door quickly opened and Missy came running toward her, arms outstretched. The two women hugged for the longest time, both with tears running down their cheeks.

"Enough with the mushy stuff," Rory said, laughter in his voice.

The women separated, and Missy playfully punched Rory on the arm and moved closer to him. "This is my best friend, Grace," she told her husband.

Grace stepped toward Rory and immediately felt dwarfed by him, as she had by Jordon. "So happy to meet you," she said. "I'm really sorry I couldn't make the wedding, but I had to work – as you know." She winked at Missy, who gave her a sly smile.

She looked around at the devastation she had caused. Her truck was badly damaged and may even be a write-off. The horse trailer appeared to have a broken axle.

All in all, an absolute disaster. She closed her eyes and contemplated where to go from here.

She flinched as Missy touched her lightly on the shoulder. "Don't worry, it will be okay. We'll come back in the morning and assess the damage."

Always the optimist was Missy. After what she'd been through – being stalked by a killer – Grace had no idea how she did it.

Missy piled her into their truck. They'd bought a horse trailer with them, following Jordon's advice, and Spirit was safely loaded in there. Grace was certain they would both enjoy some precious sleep.

* * *

Morning came too soon for Grace.

She'd only managed a few hours sleep after they'd settle Spirit into one of the stalls in Rory's stables.

She'd insisted on giving Spirit a rub down, to help ease his anxiety, and refused Rory's offer of having one of his stable hands do it for her.

Spirit was *her* horse, and *her* responsibility. He'd been with her for nearly ten years, and there was no way she would shirk her responsibility now. Not when he really needed her.

The accident must have been really terrifying for him. One minute they're driving along at a steady pace on a smooth road, then next she's down a ditch and he's on a precarious angle pushed against the side of the trailer.

She shuddered just thinking about what could have happened. It was pure luck that her beautiful boy was not injured.

Without warning, her eyes filled with tears. Shock? Or maybe the thought of losing her precious Spirit. They'd been through a lot together over the years. The good and the bad, mostly good.

Grace heard a tentative knock on the door. She quickly brushed her tears away.

"Morning!" Missy was way too bright for her liking.

She groaned as she sat up in bed. "What time is it?" Grace asked. "It feels like I've had almost no sleep." She rubbed her eyes with her fingers, and tried to block out the light coming through the door.

"It's almost noon," Missy told her, as she passed over a cup of tea. "You've missed the best part of the day already." She smiled as she teased her friend. "Jordon will be over after lunch. He wants to check Spirit out again to ensure he didn't miss anything last night."

Grace knew he had a kind heart, and this just proved it.

"Drink your tea, and get up when you're ready." Missy headed for the door. "Oh, and the shower is down the hall if you want it. Everything you need is there." And with that, she was gone.

Grace sipped her tea as she took in the view from her window. She couldn't wait to get outside and check out the view of the Montana mountains in the distance.

Missy had told her how beautiful it was, and she wanted to see for herself.

* * *

"There are definitely no breaks, but he flinched when I touched him this morning." Jordon pushed his cowboy hat back on his head. "I want to eliminate any fractures."

Grace put her hands to her mouth. "Oh no!" She was terrified of Spirit being injured. And it was all her fault. Driving through the night when she should have stopped and slept. Her eyes filled with tears. She wiped furiously at them, trying to stave the tears away.

Jordon moved toward her. "It's just a precaution, I promise." He put his arm around her shoulder and she immediately felt comforted. "It might be just bruising, but I'd rather be certain." He smiled and she felt reassured.

He went out to his truck and came back wearing a lead apron and carrying a portable x-ray machine. "Okay, you need to go outside the stall. Don't want you getting radiation poisoning." He waved her out as he set up the machine.

A short time later, Spirit was given the all-clear. "It's only bruising, no breaks or fractures. I'm going to rub some liniment into his leg and I'll check on him again tomorrow."

After he cleaned himself up, and packed his equipment away, they headed for the kitchen, where Missy had prepared an early afternoon tea. Blueberry muffins and hot beverages.

"Since when were you domesticated," Grace asked, a big grin on her face. Try as she might, she couldn't stop herself.

Missy and Rory locked eyes. "Since she became a country lady," Rory answered. There's nothing for miles around, an hour's drive to the nearest main town, so you have to do for yourself." He chuckled and Missy punched his shoulder.

"Not that he'd admit it, but Rory was my teacher. He can whip a meal or muffins up in a flash. Cakes too."

Grace took a bite out of a muffin. "Yuummy!" she said. "You'll have to teach me."

Missy's look was questioning. "How long are you staying? I mean, you can stay as long as you want, but what about work?" She stared at Grace, daring her not to answer.

Grace fidgeted in her seat. "I quit," she said quietly.

"No!" Missy jumped up from her seat. "You never!"

"I sure did," Grace told her. "For good this time." She looked down into her lap. "There's no going back this time."

As she sat back down, a thought came to Missy. "Did you win?" she asked, her voice just above a whisper.

"Sure did. A cool mil." Her smile was endless. The two women stood and ran toward each other, arms opened, tears flowing.

The two men looked confused.

"So what are you going to do now?" Missy asked. "There's no work around here."

"Sure there's work," Rory interjected. "There's lots of work, particularly seasonal work."

Missy turned to Rory. "You have no idea what you're talking about," she said sarcastically.

"There is no work for female bull riders around here."

Both men looked at each other, then at the two women, their mouths open in shock.

"Bull rider?" They said in unison.

Jordon stared into Grace's eyes. "Really? You're a bad-ass bull rider?" The laughter in his voice was priceless.

"I *was*," she answered. "But I'm not anymore."

* * *

Three days had passed, and Spirit seemed to be back to normal.

On advice from Jordon, Grace was walking him slowly around the paddocks, to keep him moving, and check for any signs of being lame.

So far so good.

They were on their third go around the pasture when Jordon arrived. He sat on the top of the fence waiting for their return.

"Howdy Ma'am," he called, as he dipped his hat.

She grinned that beautiful big grin he'd come to love.

"Howdy yourself," she shouted back, then headed toward him. He followed her to the stables, where she began to give Spirit a vigorous rub-down.

The horse was loving every minute of it. Jordon was sure he'd enjoy a rub-down from Grace as well.

He shook his head. Where the heck had that come from? He'd only known her a few days, and he was having unwanted erotic thoughts about her?

He closed his eyes trying to chase the image out of his head, but all he managed to do was inhale her vanilla perfume more intensely.

"Damn it!" He hadn't meant to say it out loud.

"You okay, cowboy?" she asked, confused.

He laughed. No one around here called him a cowboy. That was reserved for Rory. And Kody, another of his brothers.

"Yeah," he said. "I had a bit of a brain fart," he said, and she laughed her tinkling laugh that he loved to hear.

Jordon shook himself. He was a professed loner and wanted to keep it that way. Between his hands-on veterinarian work, and the mountains of paperwork he had to process, he just didn't have the time for a relationship.

Hang on! Who mentioned a relationship? You've only just met the woman a few days ago.

As much as he was coming to like Grace, he definitely wasn't interested in a relationship. Especially one that was long-term.

She stopped brushing Spirit and looked up at him. A coy little smile crossed her lips.

Oh Lordy. This was heading in a direction he simply didn't want to go.

"Come to dinner with me?" he asked, then winced. *What happened to not wanting a relationship?*

"I, I'm not sure," she said, her face suddenly serious. "I'm on the rebound." She looked down at the ground and spoke quietly. "Actually, that's a no. A rebound relationship would not be fair on you."

This was good. He didn't want a relationship anyway, right? So why did he feel so darned bad?

"Forget I ever mentioned it," he said, disappointment clearly in his voice. And with that, he walked toward his truck and left for home.

Chapter Two

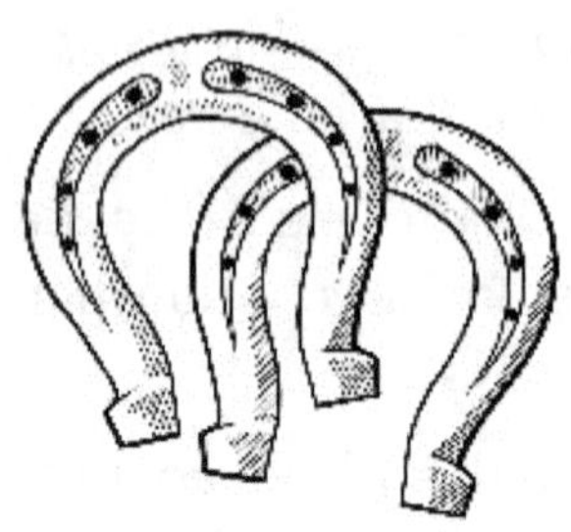

Grace lay in bed contemplating her day.

Over the years she'd invested all her bull riding prize money, and along with her latest win, she now she had a nice little nest egg.

It was beyond time to put down roots, and she wanted to be near her closest friend.

She'd met Missy when she first joined the rodeo many years ago. She was the only person to befriend Grace for quite a long time.

They were both loners but they clicked. As horse lovers, they had that in common, and often went for long slow rides in the countryside.

Their closeness was often the one thing that kept them going. Succeeding in what was predominately a man's world was not an easy task.

She suddenly jumped out of bed. Enough of this slacking around, and freeloading off her friend.

Today she would search for her forever home. Right here in River Valley.

* * *

Grace sat at the kitchen table talking to her friend while sipping a hot cup of coffee.

"I know I can stay here indefinitely," Grace said. "But it's really not an option. You two newlyweds need your space, and I need to put down roots." She looked directly into Missy's eyes, daring her to object.

"You're right of course, but I'm going to miss you," Missy said, looking sad.

"Silly, I'm not going far. I *am* looking in the River Valley area."

Missy squealed with joy.

"That's more like it," Grace said, smiling. "We've been apart for way too long, and I've been lost with out you." She covered Missy's hand with her own and squeezed it. "Fingers crossed I can find the perfect place to live."

Buddy, Rory's black and white border collie came running in, barking, trying to gain attention.

"What's wrong, boy?" Missy asked.

Rory came out of his office. "What's up boy?" Buddy headed for the front paddock, Rory and the women hot on his heels.

It was not like Buddy to behave in this way, so something was definitely up.

"Damn it, grab the rifle," Rory demanded. "It's a damned rattlesnake. Close to the horses too." He ran toward the stables, calling for one of his ranch hands. "Pete! Pete! Get the horses in the stables. There's a rattlesnake in the paddock!"

As Missy ran for the rifle, Grace, Rory and Pete each herded the horses into the stables, keeping well clear of the snake.

Grace breathed a sigh of relief when all three horses were safely tucked away. She began to check Spirit for any sigh of a snake bite, although she knew it was rare for horses to be killed by rattlesnakes. But it could still be deadly depending on where they were bitten.

"Let me deal with the snake," he said, taking the rifle from Missy. She was shaking, and Grace hugged her.

She jumped as the rifle shot rang out.

"He's done for," Rory said as he entered the stables. "I'll get Jordon out here to check the horses over. Then Pete and I will do a thorough search of that paddock. We don't want any more nasty surprises." He reached down and patted the dog. "Good boy, Buddy," he said, reaching into his pocket for a doggy treat. "God only knows what would have happened without you."

He kneeled down and rubbed the collie behind the ears, one of Buddy's favorite spots to be petted.

For a working dog, he could be a real softie.

* * *

Pete and Rory checked out the paddock and gave it the all-clear.

Jordon arrived soon after. He meticulously checked all the horses, including Spirit. They were all perfectly fine, with not even the hint of a snake bit.

Grace gave a huge sigh of relief.

"I don't know how I can ever thank you," she told Jordon. "Spirit is very special to me." She rubbed her fingers down the horse's neck as she spoke. "I don't know what I'd do without him," she said, her voicing breaking.

He pulled a carrot from his pocket and gave it to the chestnut, who gobbled it up appreciatively.

"It's my day off…" Jordon said.

"Oh, I'm so sorry!" Grace was sad they'd spoiled his plans.

He brushed his hand through the air. "Nah, don't stress over it. I just wondered if you'd like to go for a drive. See some of the area," he offered.

"Sure, why not. I'd planned on looking for some property, but I'm stuck until my truck is fixed." She hated not having her truck to get around. She loved her independence, but Missy and Rory had been fabulous, taking her wherever she needed to be.

"That's settled then."

Jordon grabbed her hand, and she felt the energy travel from her hand and up her arm. She looked directly into his eyes, which were opened wide. Did he feel it too?

"Go grab a jacket," he said, seemingly unscathed. "No idea how long we'll be, and the afternoons can get a bit chilly out here."

Just being near this man gave her a warm fuzzy feeling. She hadn't felt this way in a very long time, even with her ex, who she thought she'd loved. Looking back, they were more like friends with benefits than what you would call lovers. There really wasn't much love there – more like they were fond of each other. Not much more.

"Come on, let's go," he called to Grace as she left the ranch house. She understood he wanted to go before the day got too late. She might even see a property or two that took her fancy.

She didn't want much – a ranch house she could call home, a few chickens, a small vegetable garden, and a place for Spirit to run free. He'd given her so much over the years, and he deserved to live out his life in peace.

* * *

Montana was beautiful.

Okay, so was Wyoming, but River Valley had that close-knit community feel to it. She'd never felt that anywhere before.

For that reason, she knew it was the place for her. Where she wanted to live. Where her forever home needed to be.

Of course, having her best friend living here made it even more appealing. Rory was fabulous, and Jordon? Well, Jordon was special.

She wasn't sure what it was about Jordon, but they connected. Not as friends though, it was on a different level. She connected with him in another way.

As much as she was not looking for a boyfriend, or a partner, she felt extremely comfortable with him. Was it the way he'd looked after Spirit? She always had a soft-spot for anyone who was kind to animals. But he'd been kind to her as well, even before he found out she knew Missy.

He was special for sure, and she was beginning to feel *too* comfortable with him. In a way she'd never experienced before. She gave herself a shake.

He glanced across as he drove. "What do you think so far?"

Grace looked at his big, strong hands. She would love to feel those hands around her, hugging her.

He turned toward her again, and her eyes locked on his lips. She licked hers, and his eyes watched every movement.

"Grace, are you okay?"

"Sorry, yeah. I love it," she said. "This is definitely where I'd like to be." She pulled her eyes from his as they waited at a crossroad. "I don't suppose you know of any properties up for sale." She tried to clear her head of thoughts of Jordon, but it was difficult.

"As a matter of fact, I do." In his travels as a vet, he came across lots of clients, and many talked to him as he worked. "It really depends on how big you want this property to be. But we'll go over there and you can take a look."

As they headed in that direction, Grace contemplated what her life would be like to finally have her own property and be close to her friend.

* * *

Joe Fisher kindly showed Grace around his property.

She thanked him and apologetically told him it was way too big for her needs. What she really wanted was akin to a hobby farm. A nice ranch house with stables and about six acres of land. That way she could raise a few chickens and potter around in the vegetable garden she planned to plant.

If it took off, she might even make it into a side business.

They were back in Jordon's truck when he had a thought. "Just an idea, but have you thought about running a riding school? You could even do trail rides," he said, glancing across at her. "There are plenty of places around here you could take a small group on horses."

She closed her eyes, thinking of the possibilities. She'd need to get at least ten horses to make that happen, but it was doable.

And six acres would still be plenty big enough, unless she decided to use her own land for the trail rides. She dismissed that idea almost the moment it hit her brain.

"You know, I think you're on to something there, Jordon."

His grin lit up his face. "Happy to be of assistance, Ma'am." He tipped his cowboy hat and turned back to the road.

Her thoughts suddenly turned in another direction. "Only problem is, that will all take time, right?" Maybe it was not going to be as easy as she first thought. "I need somewhere *now*. I don't want to keep freeloading off Rory and Missy, and as newlyweds, they definitely need their own space."

Jordon pulled to the side of the road. "Here's a plan." He took her hands in his, and his warmth engulfed her immediately. "We can go to the local real estate office and find out what's available. Then..."

She was shaking her head. "Still going to take forever."

"How quickly do you need this property?" Jordon asked. "I mean, do you need to set everything up right away, or do you just want to leave my brother and his wife alone?"

"Mostly the latter. I need somewhere to stay more than anything. Money is not an issue. If I could find somewhere temporary while I search for the perfect property, I'd be more than happy."

Jordon was thinking. She could almost see his brain ticking over. Then suddenly his eyes widened.

"Aha! I think I may have solved one of your problems. Want to check it out?" He looked thoroughly pleased with himself.

"Um, yes, I guess so," she replied, not sure what she was getting herself into.

Jordon took his hands away to start the engine, and she felt hollow. As much as she liked Jordon, she was happy to be friends, but she wasn't prepared to go any further than that.

If she kept telling herself, she might start believing it.

* * *

"It's off the beaten track, I'll grant you that, but it's a nice little cottage." They had arrived at a rundown *shack*, definitely not a cottage in her opinion.

"It belonged to my great grandparents, but as you can see, it's not been lived in for a very long time. Apparently great grandmother Bessie had some sort of secret, but we're yet to uncover it."

Grace contemplated his words as she looked at the dust and grime. "Uh-huh. But what does that have to do with me?" Was he out of his mind? This place wasn't even habitable in its current state. "Who does it belong to anyway?"

"It's mine. This cottage is on my property. My great grandfather owned all the property belonging to me and my brothers. It was subdivided after our grandfather died. Our parents were killed in a riding accident many years ago, and he brought us up."

"I'm so sorry," Grace said quietly. She had no idea.

Jordon waved his hands at her. "It was a long time ago now. Anyway, you can stay here if you'd like. I'll help you clean it up when I'm available." He pushed his hat back on his head. "Country vet. You know, always on call."

"It looks like it's sat empty for decades." Or maybe a hundred years. But she wouldn't voice that opinion!

"It has. For as long as I can remember it's been empty. Grandfather built the house I live in now, and moved in there after he began to care for my brothers and me. This cottage only has a few bedrooms, and there are four brothers," he said.

"I've had big plans for this place, but never got around to it."

Grace looked around. What could you do here but live in it? "Plans? What were you planning to do here?" No matter what he did, there would be a ton of work involved.

"I'd like to turn it into an animal hospital. Right now I only look after farm animals. I'd like to branch out and treat pets as well. Locals are going to Boulton for domestic animals, when they could come here."

"So why offer it to me?" Grace was confused. Why indeed?

"Because I simply don't have the time to do it. It's a future plan." He looked a little deflated, but perhaps her staying here, sprucing it up a little, might get his plans back on track.

It would take a bit of work, but Grace was sure this little cottage would suit her needs. And there was a stable. A small stable that would only take a couple of horses, but still it would work for now.

"Do I get to use one of the paddocks too?" she asked. She needed somewhere for Spirit to run free. She shivered when she thought of the rattle snake that had invaded Rory and Missy's property earlier today.

"Of course. You can use as much of the property as you want. It all attaches to my ranch house, but I don't use much of it, so go for it."

"Okay, down to business," Grace said. "How much rent?" She didn't want to pay too much, but had to pay her way.

"Nada. If you clean it up and make it presentable, that will be enough payment for me. And you can stay as long as you like. It's just sitting empty after all." Jordon looked around and ran his fingers through the dust on a nearby table. "This was all their furniture you know. All handmade. My grandfather was born in this house, it has a lot of history."

Grace walked over and took his dusty hands in hers. "I love this place," she said quietly. "And I'd love to bring it back to its former glory." He smiled and she wondered if he was imagining how it used to be, as she was.

Children running around feeding, or maybe chasing, the chickens, horses in the paddocks, and maybe some cows in the paddocks grazing.

She pulled herself out of her revelry. "Done!" She shook Jordon's hand and made a pact to clean the place up.

* * *

"I'm so excited for you!" Missy squealed with joy. She was so happy for her friend. "I've heard all about that little cottage. I've only seen it from afar, mind you, so you'll have to show me!"

Grace was frowning. She knew she was. It had finally hit her how much work was involved in getting the cottage back to a usable condition. Had it really been empty for nearly one hundred years? She'd probably never know.

"Before I can do anything, I'm going to have to go into town and buy a bucket load of cleaning supplies. It's going to take forever to get rid of the dust, let alone anything else that might be lurking there."

"Eeeewww!"

"Oh my God," Grace said. "What if there are dead rats in there? Or, heaven forbid, live rats." Now she felt ill.

The look of horror on Missy's face confirmed her greatest fears, that she could just be right.

"No. No, no, no. Please tell me it isn't true." Her eyes implored Missy to deny it, but neither woman knew the truth.

"Hey, come on," Missy suddenly announced. "You're tough, you're a bull rider. You're not going to let a little mouse rattle you, are you?"

"Mice I can deal with, but rats?" She gave a little shudder. "Rats are the pits. Hate them with a vengeance. They are filthy little beasts who will bite anything and anyone.

"I know," Missy said, quite animated now. "I'll get Rory to give it the once over." She was grinning by now, despite the fact Grace was sure she was serious.

"Get Rory to what?" the man himself asked. "Hopefully nothing too time consuming," he said, putting his cowboy hat firmly on his head as he exited the house.

"Get rid of any rats in the old cottage," Missy called after him.

"Rats," he said. "We use pest control for that," he answered absent mindedly, then walked toward the stables.

The two women glanced at each other. "Of course!" Grace said, then turned to her phone looking for local companies.

"Begone, ye old rats," Missy said, as she grinned at her friend.

* * *

The more Grace saw him, the more attracted to Jordon she became.

It was not something she welcomed, especially after a nasty break-up, and also when she was trying to find herself after retiring from bull-riding.

She'd been on the circuit for her entire adult life, and had been involved with rodeos before that. Her father introduced her to the rodeo life when she was still in junior school, and she couldn't get it out of her mind.

As a teenager, she decided she wanted to be a bull-rider, after watching the burly men riding. Everyone laughed when she said that's what she wanted to do, because understandably, it is a man's world.

She had the injuries to prove it.

Not to say women can't endure them, because she proved otherwise, but the female body wasn't made to endure that sort of treatment. She spent more than half her bull-riding career taped up in some way.

She rubbed her hands across her shoulder. It still ached, even after a few weeks, and especially now with all this cleaning. Thank goodness she'd come to her senses and decided to retire from that life.

"Hey, you okay?" Jordon's voice brought her back to reality.

She glanced up to see him staring at her, a frown furrowing his brow. "Yeah, sure. Just thinking about my life on the circuit."

He stepped toward her, and brushed some dirt from her cheek. She could feel the warmth coming from his body, and she wanted to be wrapped in his arms.

What...? Where did that come from? What happened to keeping your distance?

Grace admonished herself. This is not what she wanted right now. She had an agenda, and she intended to stick to it.

Jordon looked at her quizzically. "You alright, darl? You look pale." This time he reached out and brushed her silky brown hair out of her face.

She stepped back. *Darl? He was getting a little too familiar.* "Sure. I'm fine. Just a little tired," she lied. *Don't get too close.*

"So let's take a break. Hey, I have a thermos of coffee in the truck. I'll go get it."

He headed outside before she could protest. Typical man of the land. Prepared for any eventuality.

She sighed as she sipped the hot brew. "That hit the spot. Thanks Jordon. I really needed that."

She smiled. Probably for the first time today. She'd worked her butt off in the cottage, but saw little results for her hard work and persistence.

Just then his pager went off. "Sorry, I have to go. Duty calls."

Suddenly he was gone, and she felt totally alone.

* * *

There was still a long way to go before the cottage would be habitable, but Grace was finally seeing some results for her efforts.

Missy had been an enormous help, and without her Grace knew there would be little change.

Tackling one room at a time, had definitely been the best way to go. The kitchen was beginning to peek through from under all that dust and grime of the past several decades.

"Can you even imagine working in this kitchen one hundred years ago?" Grace said.

Missy screwed up her face. "It must have been awful. Really hard work."

Since there was no electricity at the cottage, they were using cold water for all the cleaning, so it was slow going.

"At least we haven't come across any rats," Missy added, voice deadpan.

"Yet." It was Jordon. He'd appeared out of nowhere, but his presence was certainly appreciated. He had made it a habit to drop in at least once a day, to see how things were progressing, he'd said.

But Grace had hoped there was more to it than that. She'd found herself thinking about Jordon more and more, despite her wishes to the contrary.

Not that he wasn't a nice guy. And he sure was a looker, but she just wasn't ready for another relationship. Especially with her best friend's brother-in-law.

That could be sticky if the relationship fell in a heap. Urgh. It didn't bear thinking about. She was not prepared to ruin her friendship with Missy. *Over a man no less!*

Jordon peeked over her shoulder at the mess in the bucket. "Yuk. There was lots of dust, yeah?"

Grace rolled her eyes. What did he expect? That the water would be clean after they'd removed the dust? Missy caught her eye, and seemed to be thinking the same.

As he moved away from her, Jordon brushed Grace's shoulder and she stood planted where she stood. Every time he was near, she felt a jolt. It was as though she'd been hit by lightening. His nearness did things to her.

He did things to her.

It was the last thing she wanted right now.

"Let me help with that," he said, taking the bucket of filthy water from her. She so wanted him to leave right now. Just being in the same room was making her feel…. Something.

She wasn't quite sure what it was she was feeling, but it wasn't how she had felt before he'd arrived.

She gazed up into his eyes. They seemed to be sparkling. Was that because of her? Or maybe the sunlight was hitting them in just the right place?

Nah, it wasn't the sun – they were standing inside the cottage.

"Coffee," he said. "I've brought coffee with me. Lots of it."

He didn't have to ask twice as both women were getting desperate. As he passed over a cup of the boiling liquid, their hands brushed, and she felt it again. A shiver went through her, and she felt the warmth from his big calloused hands.

Jordon was a man of the land, a lover of animals, and an all-round good guy. She could certainly fall hard for him if she let herself.

Trouble was, did she trust herself to get close to this man who made her feel all sorts of things that she wasn't quite ready to feel?

* * *

Grace didn't want to think about how many hours she had already spent cleaning out the cottage.

It was an adventure for sure, and it *would* be a cozy place to live once it was finished.

Missy had just put on the kettle when Grace had found it. "Missy! Quick! Come here."

Her friend came running. "Are you okay?" she asked, a worried look on her face.

"Sorry. Yes, I'm fine," Grace told her friend. "But I think I've found something. A secret compartment perhaps." She indicated what looked like a small square door. It was built into the corner of one wall in the tiny sitting room.

"What is it?" Missy asked, looking as dumbfounded as Grace felt.

"No idea. But I think we're going to need a crowbar or something similar to try and force this open."

Missy looked at her in shock. "Really?" she said. "Maybe we should just leave it alone." She pouted, and Grace, knowing her friend as she did, knew she didn't really want to leave it.

The pair went out to Missy's truck and found a crowbar. They spent the next fifteen minutes trying to force the hidden door open. Finally it gave way.

Dust flew up in the air, and they both began to cough. Grace flung her hands in the air trying to disburse the dust.

They both stared in the cavity before them. There was a very ragged looking book hidden in the previously concealed cavity.

"What is it?" Missy whispered.

"Why are you whispering?" Grace asked. They both laughed.

"Yew, look at the spider webs. I'm not putting my hands in there," Missy wailed.

"Rubber gloves," Grace said, pulling them onto her hands.

Jordon arrived as they pulled the tattered book from the wall. "Look what we found!" Grace said excitedly. "Do you want to do the honors?" It was his great-grandparents home after all.

It was a diary. Great grandmother Bessie's diary.

Jordon began to read from it.

May 8, 1880

"My eighteenth birthday was only a few months ago. It was a joyous occasion, and my parents held a coming out party for me. I was presented to several eligible young men, and my father had high hopes that I would marry one of them. One young man particularly caught his eye as his family was fabulously rich, but he was not to my standards. The stench that came from him was almost unbearable."

June 19, 1880

"Why must father pursue that wretched man? Every time he comes to the house, I nearly faint from his putrid odor. All father can see is his family's money. He says I will be well looked after. What I see is a life of misery."

July 10, 1880.

"It is a very sad day for me. My uncle came to me to advise both my parents were killed in a coach accident. My uncle has been given everything, including our house, as I am underage. I have no idea what I am going to do now."

It was written in the most beautiful cursive handwriting Grace had ever seen.

"WOW," Jordon said. "I didn't know any of that. I don't think any of us knew."

July 15, 1880

"On the advice of my uncle, I traveled to Hudson Montana to take up a position as a singer, but it would turn out to be the worst thing I could ever have done. For a time, I was angry at my parents for dying, but understood that was unreasonable. I also blamed my uncle, but he could never have known what I was about to endure."

"Oh my gosh," Jordon said as his pager went off. "This is going to be interesting, but I have to go," he said, looking at the two women. "But you two go ahead."

"Oh no," said Grace. "We can't do that – it's a family heirloom. Family must be the first to read it. You take it." She knew it was the right thing to do, but Grace would have loved to read more.

She wrapped the ancient diary in a table cloth to protect it, and handed it to Jordon.

She desperately wanted to read more, but Jordon and his family must be the first to read it. That was their right.

Chapter Three

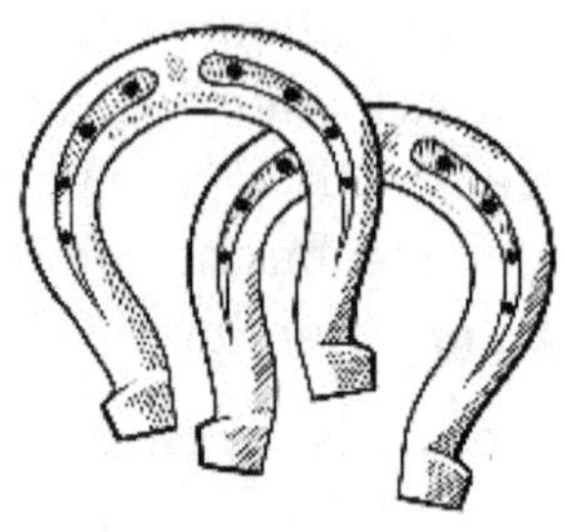

Jordon had a rare day off.

At least he hoped he did — he was always on call. Being the only vet in the area sometimes took its toll, but he loved his job. Especially when he knew he made a difference to his patients. His animal patients that is.

He was going to drop into the cottage to see how things were going there, but decided not to after all.

He felt a strange pull toward Grace, which was the total opposite to what he'd intended. He was happy to have her as a friend, but nothing more.

Past relationships had not turned out so well. Most women didn't understand that call-outs and emergencies could happen at absolutely any time of the day. Or night.

Just like it did with human patients.

And then there was his last relationship. That ended in disaster. He shook his head. He didn't want to think about any of it.

He had decided to take a drive up into the mountains. Maybe the air up there might help to clear his head? Maybe it could exorcise Grace from his mind completely?

Highly unlikely, but worth a try.

That woman was stuck there firmly, and no matter what he did, he could not get her out. He thought of her night and day, and little things triggered memories of her.

Not that he knew her all that well. Grace seemed to be distancing herself from him.

Much like he was doing to her, he mused.

He continued his leisurely drive up the windy road toward the peak. One of his favorite places to be was at the look-out up the top. From there he could see the whole area for miles around.

It was always peaceful there and helped him put his thoughts in order.

After arriving at his destination, he stood at the look-out. He could see the cottage from there. It was all but a tiny dot from this distance. But he knew Grace would be there.

What was she doing? Was she alone or was Missy there with her?

He shook himself. Why did his thoughts always turn back to Grace? It was apparent to Jordon that Grace wasn't the least bit interested in him as man. More as a friend.

45

And that was far from what his body was telling him he wanted to be.

* * *

Grace needed fresh air.

Not only was it dusty in there, it was stuffy. And stifling.

She was alone today. She knew Missy wouldn't be able to help out every day. Since marrying Rory, Missy had cut down her hours at the Bar and Grill, where she was a singer.

A far cry from her days as a rodeo stunt rider.

It was as though she was born to be on the stage. And she loved it.

She had to work tonight, so she was unable to come over and help. Her friend gave her all to whatever she did, and tonight that was her stage performance.

It was funny, because before Missy had left Wyoming, Grace had only ever known her as a stunt rider. There was a whole other side to her friend that had been hidden away.

When she walked outside, her gaze locked on the stables. They needed to be in good condition because when she eventually moved into the cottage, Spirit would come with her.

There was no way she would leave her beloved horse behind. They'd been inseparable for years, and that was the way it would stay.

Grace brushed back the hair from her face. Her hands were left covered in cobwebs. "Yuk. No, no, no!" she shouted, brushing the filthy things out of her hair.

Were there any spiders there too? Her heart beat rapidly as she contemplated the thought. Rats and spiders. Her pet hates. She shuddered as she ran her fingers through her cobweb-ridden hair.

If Jordon were here, he'd make sure nothing was there.

Jordon.

Why did her thoughts always turn to him? She'd already decided to keep her distance. He was far from interested. And Grace? Well, she wasn't certain what she wanted beyond a place of her own. A place where she could lay her head at night.

At least there was electricity connected. Apparently Jordon had organised that some years ago, but it had never been turned on.

Oh my. Why didn't she think of that before? Turning on the electricity so she could have hot water for the cleaning. She shook her head in despair.

She made a mental note to organise that tomorrow.

Grace went into the stables. They were nowhere near as bad as the cottage. She moved the stall doors back and forth. They appeared to be usable.

Of course, she'd need to give them a spruce up, and get some hay, but in day or two they should be perfectly livable.

She pictured Spirit here. She could see him enjoying himself running through the adjourning paddock, his mane flying through the air on a windy day. And she could see herself riding him around the property.

As Grace was caught up in her thoughts, she reveled in the quiet. The total respite from the city, where she'd been living the last how many years? Too many in her opinion.

She'd been such a fool to begin a career as a bull rider, let alone continue with it. Her body had been damaged to a point she was often in pain doing the most menial tasks.

Grace turned to leave the stables and saw a silhouette of a man in the distance.

She called out. "Jordon? Is that you?" Instead of responding, the man ran. Quickly.

Grace gasped. *If it wasn't Jordon, who was it?* She stood frozen where she stood. Heart beating rapidly. She hugged herself tightly and stared into the distance in disbelief.

She could feel herself shaking, but she couldn't move, she was so afraid.

Since she'd moved to River Valley Montana she hadn't had to worry. But it seems he had found her.

What was she going to do now?

* * *

Jordon arrived at the cottage knowing full well Grace would be there. She wanted to move in as quickly as possible, and had spent just about every waking moment there.

He was torn, because he couldn't abandon his practice to help her, and knew if he'd done what he'd intended some years ago, the place would be in a much better state.

But his clients and their animals had to come first.

He'd bought a picnic lunch with him, with all the trimmings. Sandwiches, cakes, and even a bottle of wine.

Missy was a gem – she'd given him some baked goods to bring along. He got the distinct impression there was some match-making going on there.

As he walked in, Grace was stretching, then rubbed her shoulders. It was obvious she was working too hard but try telling her that.

"Good morning." He stood in the doorway as he announced his presence.

Grace spun around, and the look of horror on her face was palpable.

"Oh my God. I'm so sorry," Jordon said. "I didn't mean to scare you."

He could see her eyes tearing up, and wondered why. He rushed toward her. "Are you okay?" He touched her shoulder, trying to comfort her, but instead felt that now familiar warmth, and a small jolt. Just like the last time he'd touched her.

She brushed at her cheeks, and it was only then he noticed a tear rolling down her face. "I'm okay. Really," she said, straightening her shoulders and forcing herself to stand taller. "I just.... didn't know you were there."

Jordon wasn't buying it. Something wasn't right.

"I brought some food. Want to go for a picnic?" He gazed into her face and smiled. She still looked scared, but it was obvious to him she wasn't going to discuss it.

"Uh,"

She was going to refuse. He knew she was.

"Missy gave me some of her blueberry muffins," he added quickly, hoping that would convince her.

Grace looked to her feet. "I have so much to do," she explained.

"Nope, nope, nope. You are coming with me. You have to eat, after all." He grabbed her hand and started to pull her out of the cottage. He felt a thrill run up his arm.

"At least let me clean up before we go," Grace told him.

He reached out and brushed the dust from her face. He shuddered. He felt so much for this stubborn woman, as much as he tried to deny it.

She stared into his face, then his eyes. His thumb moved to her lips, and he brushed his thumb across her bottom lip.

She stood there, rooted to the spot, not saying a word.

Her tongue suddenly flicked out and touched his thumb. He swallowed.

He moved closer to her, and licked his lips. His head went closer, seemingly of its own volition. He surely hadn't done that.

His eyes met hers. She seemed to be saying yes, but his brain kept saying *no, don't do it. Stay away.*

He took a deep breath then backed away. *What had he been thinking?* "Righto then, get washed up and we'll be on our way."

* * *

As much as she wanted to be back in the cottage cleaning up, Grace was enjoying the break.

The fresh air was energizing, calming, and just what she needed.

Jordon had taken them in his off-road vehicle through one of the paddocks, and down to a small stream that ran through his property.

She'd taken a deep breath, and she could smell the vegetation. It was so unlike the city out here. Jordon had laid a picnic blanket near the stream, next to a Western Snowberry for shade.

It had pretty little pink flowers that Grace adored.

She walked over to the stream while Jordon set up their picnic. She was so glad he talked her into this. She really needed a break.

She knelt and ran her fingers through the cool water of the stream. A school of fish swam by and she smiled. Such a simple thing to do, but it gave her so much pleasure.

The light breeze sent her long hair flying across her face, and she laughed.

"What's so funny?" She hadn't even heard him walk toward her. Not necessarily a good thing.

"Oh, the fresh air. The breeze. Even the cool water running through my fingers," she said, as she watched his smile travel from his lips to his eyes. "I even saw some rainbow trout!" She felt like a child again, but her feelings for Jordon were far from child-like.

As she turned toward him, she hadn't realized how close his face was to hers. She licked her lips and looked into his sparkling brown eyes.

Her heart was saying yes, but her brain was saying no. Her body was saying for sure, but her common sense was saying this was the craziest idea she'd had for a long time.

Despite herself, Grace moved slowly toward him. They were face to face, lips almost touching. His hand came up and brushed against her cheek. Her eyes closed.

She knew that was a fatal mistake, but she moved closer to him despite her misgivings.

His thumb moved across her lips, then his lips gently brushed hers. Both hands cupped her face, and he tilted his head.

She heard herself groan, and then she was lost.

* * *

Missy had decided to have a family dinner.

She didn't do it often, but Jordon decided she was match-making again.

Although he'd shared a kiss with Grace, that was as far as it had gone. Not that he was complaining. He wanted to take it slowly.

He'd been burned before. Badly burned.

The day he was to walk down the aisle.

His soon-to-be wife had decided she didn't want to be a veterinarian's wife, to live in the wide-open spaces. She wanted to live in the city instead.

She phoned him one hour before the wedding.

And that was that.

But Grace was different. She loved the country. She loved animals. And he hoped she would eventually love him.

He wasn't sure yet if he loved Grace. There was certainly something between them. Chemistry, and something more.

He heard the tinkling of her laughter coming from inside the house. Most likely the kitchen, where Missy had been teaching her how to cook — when time was available.

She looked up as he walked through the door, and it was as though time stood still. He stared into her face. They shared a secret no one else knew.

He reached out for her, then stopped himself.

His entire damned family didn't need to know his business.

"How is the whole cleaning the cottage thing going?" He knew, of course he knew. He was there today, with Grace. Holding her in his arms. Kissing her madly. Not wanting to let her go.

She fiddled with her hands. "Oh. Fine," she said, then smiled conspiratorially.

Missy stared at them. Did she know? Had Grace told her? *No, she wouldn't. Missy had guessed.* Jordon put his fingers to his lips.

She slowly walked toward him. "Your secret is safe with me," she whispered, then looked into his eyes momentarily and sauntered away. A smile on her face.

All three of Rory's brothers had been invited. It was an opportunity for the others to meet Grace, Missy had told him. Only Jordon didn't want his other brothers to meet her. Not yet.

What if they decided to fight him for her?

Jordon shook himself. Now he was being stupid. It was early days. Hell, they'd had one kiss. Okay, maybe more than one kiss!

His brother Kody walked through the door. "Bro! Howdy." Kody extended his hand and gave his brother a man-hug.

Kody had sworn off women a long time ago, but that didn't mean he couldn't or wouldn't change his mind.

"Glad you could come, Kody," Missy said, hugging him. "This is my friend, Grace," she told him. He turned to face the newcomer, and smiled. His eyes moved up and down her body, and Jordon was ready to slug him.

He heard an off-road vehicle pull up and knew it would be Chase, his other brother.

Chase was a little more cautious than even Jordon. His wife had been killed in a car accident twelve months after they'd married.

56

It had been a sad time for them all.

"Okay, foods up!" Missy announced, herding them all toward a trestle table out the back. There was a variety of barbequed meats, salads, bread rolls, and more.

Desserts would come out later.

Jordon grabbed two plates and headed toward Grace. He spotted Missy watching him. She knew. She definitely knew. Her sly smile told him so.

He handed Grace a plate and put a hand to her back, guiding her over to the table. She took a little of everything and followed him back to the chairs, which had been placed in a circle.

For a very long time their family had been just the brothers and their grandfather. After he'd died, it was just the boys.

They'd always been close, but when they lost their grandfather, they became closer still.

"Jordon," Grace said quietly. "Are you okay?"

He'd been lost in thought. "Yeah, sure. Just thinking," he answered.

"Grace is fixing up the old cottage," Missy offered to anyone who was willing to listen.

"WOW, that's fabulous," Chase answered. "But why would you do that?" He looked confused.

Jordon answered, trying to take the focus off Grace. He didn't want his brothers to stake a claim on her. "She needed a place to stay, I offered the cottage," he said. "And I get it cleaned free in the process." He laughed at his own joke.

The rest of the night proceeded at a friendly banter, but there was always at least one of his brothers around. Jordon was itching to get Grace alone.

Longed to feel her arms around him again, and ached for her kiss.

* * *

Missy sat atop Mishka, her horse, and Grace rode Spirit.

They had decided to go for a short ride.

Grace loved the open spaces of River Valley, and longed to feel the wind in her hair. She'd worked hard on the cottage, and it was nearly done.

The pest controller had rid the cottage of it's family of rats, and she felt more comfortable there now.

Next on the agenda was to buy a bed and some bedding, as well as some easy chairs, and maybe a small television.

Once she'd mapped out her plan for a horse-riding school, she'd need an office, so a desk would be next.

She loved her new abode, and reveled in the fact she'd be living there in a matter of days. Without Missy and Jordon, it wouldn't have happened.

She breathed a deep and clarifying sigh.

"Yeah, I know that feeling," Missy said. "It's like that sometimes."

Grace leaned forward and lay against Spirit's neck, patting the horse's head. "It sure is," Grace responded. "I'm not sure if I said it before, but thank you for all the help you've given me." She reached over and held Missy's hand. "I really appreciate it."

"If you appreciate it so much," Missy said smiling, "Tell me what's going on with you and Jordon."

Grace rolled her eyes. "Nothing," she said. Missy stared open mouthed. "Okay, a little. We've had one teensy little kiss," Grace said. "And maybe a hug or two."

"Don't you go hurting that man," Missy told her. "He's been through enough already."

"What the hell, Missy! You know I wouldn't hurt anyone intentionally." Grace was annoyed. What a terrible thing to say.

Then she frowned. "What do you mean that he's been through enough?" Her interest was piqued now, but she knew it really wasn't her business.

"Jilted an hour before his wedding, I was told," Missy explained. "Horrible. Just horrible. Poor Jordon."

WOW. She didn't expect that. Jordon hadn't mentioned it, but why should he? They'd only recently met, and it wasn't as though they were lovers. They barely knew each other.

Grace climbed down from Spirit. "I just need to stretch a little," she said. "That old bull fighting injury has caught up with me," she told Missy. She reached into her pocket and pulled out two carrots, feeding one to Spirit, and handing one to her friend for Mishka.

"What the……? Did you see that?" Missy asked, astounded.

Grace was confused. "See what?" She hadn't seen anything. They were in the middle of nowhere. Then she realized. Surely he hadn't followed them out here? It wasn't enough that he was stalking her, now he was putting her friend's life in danger too?

"It looked like a man in the distance."

Grace was upset and furious, and felt the heat creep up her face. "We should go," she said abruptly. Her friend looked confused but nodded her acquiesce.

They were soon on their way home, Grace glancing over her shoulder as they rode.

Chapter Four

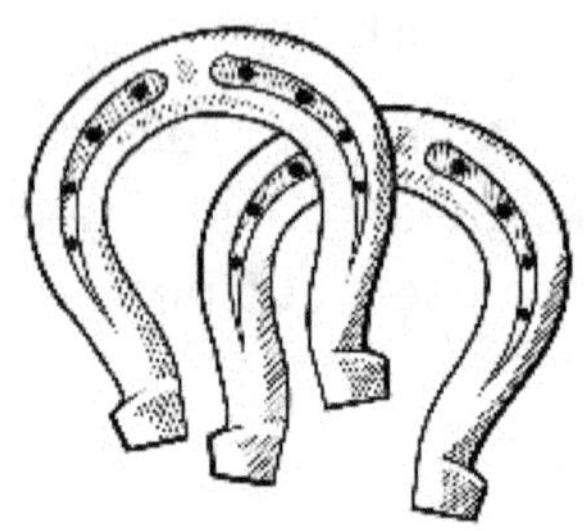

Jordon had invited Grace out for dinner.

There weren't many places in River Valley where you could have a quiet date, but Aunt Lizzie's Kitchen was one. All hustle and bustle during the day, but at night? A totally different atmosphere.

Aunt Lizzie – or Lizzie to everyone in town – made everything from scratch. There wasn't a store-bought product to be found anywhere in the building.

She prided herself on fresh.

Grace was a jeans and shirt kind of gal, but tonight she'd dressed up to the nines. Jordon hoped it was for him.

She wore a white off the shoulder lace top, that had flowing ribbons hanging from the sleeves. The skirt she wore matched in color, and was pleated at the front, but only in the middle. It had a panel of embroidery to one side, and came to just below her knees.

She finished it off with pale pink sandals that accented her dainty feet. Her long flowing hair, styled with a light curl, finished off the look.

Jordon was impressed.

Lizzie stood next to them at the table. She'd given them a quiet spot, tucked away at the back of the restaurant. "Who is this young lady you're wining and dining tonight, young Jordon?"

Even though it probably meant nothing, Jordon flinched. As the youngest of the four boys, he used to always cop flack about being the youngest Callahan.

"Not so young now, Aunt Lizzie," he said. He'd always called her aunt, and out of respect, probably always would. "I'm thirty-one years old, in case you didn't know."

Grace laughed and he felt the heat creep up his face.

She leaned over and shook Aunt Lizzie's hand. "Grace Black," she said. "I'm a friend of Missy Callahan's. Very pleased to meet you."

"What can I get for you, Grace?" Lizzie asked, totally disregarding Jordon for now. She always looked after the ladies first.

"There's too much here to choose from," Grace said, apparently overwhelmed by the menu.

"If you want something light, we do a lovely warm chicken salad," Lizzie said. "Or for something heavier, we have steak and veg, with whatever sauce your heart desires. For dessert, we have pancakes with strawberries and ice-cream, or there's freshly made apple pie."

She winked at Grace, and then looked at Jordon. "Or you might prefer your fella over there."

Jordon felt the heat crawl up his face again, only this time, for an entirely different reason.

Lizzie eventually took their orders and was on her way.

"I love her!" Grace exclaimed, after Lizzie was out of earshot.

Jordon sighed. "Yeah, apart from embarrassing me in front of my dates, she's a good old bird."

When they'd finished their dinner, they ordered coffee, but Jordon was anxious to leave. To be alone with Grace.

They chatted over their coffee, and he told her how he'd originally planned to use the cottage for a veterinarian clinic. Domestic animals.

There was nowhere close to River Valley that looked after domestic pets, such as cats and dog, birds and other small creatures. People had to travel for over an hour for the nearest vet. He didn't want it to become the biggest part of his business, far from it, but he wanted to be able to help out the locals. Especially when there was an emergency.

He watched the color drain out of Grace's face. "Oh no!" he said. "Don't stress. That plan is way down the track. If at all."

"Phew!" she said. "For a minute there I thought I was going to be homeless again." She smiled tentatively.

Jordon reached over and held her hand. "Sorry. I didn't mean to spoil your night." Now he felt like a jerk.

"You didn't. I just over reacted." Her cheeks were a rosy pink again, and Jordon breathed a sigh of relief.

He leaned in and whispered in her ear. "Let's get out of here. I know a quiet little place…"

They were both standing before he had the chance to finish his sentence.

* * *

Jordon paid the bill for their meal and led her out to his truck.

"It's nearly dark, but there's a place I'd like to take you," he said as he started the engine. "Trust me enough to go without knowing where it is?"

Grace took a deep breath. "Sure." She hadn't known Jordon for all that long, but if Missy trusted him, she trusted him.

And her gut was telling her that Jordon was one of the good guys.

He drove out of town and toward the windy road that led to the mountains that overlooked River Valley.

She'd heard it was beautiful up there. That you could look down over the valley and see for miles around. But you had to be in the right place to do it.

Hopefully that was where Jordon was taking her.

She felt a little lightheaded with excitement, and her heart rate had accelerated. She stared out the truck window and saw the lights of River Valley. It was so pretty. But not as pretty as she was sure it would be when it was darker, and they were higher up the mountain.

Jordon reached over and squeezed her hand. "You okay, over there?" he asked, taking his eyes off the road momentarily.

"Just enjoying the view," Grace answered. "It is so beautiful."

"Wait until we arrived. Then tell me how beautiful it is." He smiled at her and her heart melted. Grace felt totally at home with this wonderful man. She was getting way too attached. What if he decided to ditch her? Would her heart survive?

Jordon suddenly slammed on the brakes. "Damn foxes," he yelled. "Sorry," he said, "but these creatures are stupid. They run out into the headlights and get themselves killed."

Luckily he'd missed this particular fox, and they were soon on their way again.

They continued driving, until Jordon came to a slow stop. He came around and opened her door, then led her to a mountain top look out. He'd obviously been here before.

Grace moved to the safety fence and looked all around her. She could see lights and tiny houses for miles around. He came up behind her and wrapped his arms around her. "Isn't it something else?" he whispered in her ear.

Just being this close sent shivers down her spine. His warm breath on her cheek made her want to kiss him, and she spun around in his arms.

She looked into his endless brown eyes, then slid her gaze to his lips. She licked hers then slowly moved closer to his face.

His arms wrapped around her tightly, and they were close. As close as they could get without being naked. She wasn't excluding that as an option somewhere down the track.

Jordon tipped his head to the side and kissed her gently. Grace wasn't having any of that, and kissed him more passionately. He took the hint and pushed his tongue into her willing mouth.

Her arms came up around his back, and she pushed her hands up inside his shirt. He felt warm, inviting, and strong. She wanted this man, and she wanted him now.

But not atop a mountain in a car. They needed to find somewhere private and comfortable.

* * *

Grace woke up in an unfamiliar bed. Then she remembered.

A smile came to her face.

She rolled over, and there was Jordon. With his back to her, only his blonde hair peeked out from under the sheet, but she knew he was stark naked under there, and beautiful.

Fully clothed she'd had no idea how taut and terrific his body was. As he'd made love to her his muscles bulged, and she'd run her hands over them.

He'd looked into her eyes and smiled. Then continued his love making. His lips connected with hers, and they kissed like they'd never kissed before.

His lips moved lower down and settled on her neck. She felt him suckle then felt a teensy sting. He'd given her a love-bite. Marking her for her brothers to see she was taken, no doubt. A tiny smile came to her face.

On reflection, Grace had no idea why she thought Jordon wasn't interested in her. None whatsoever.

This wasn't lust. Sure they wanted each other almost from the moment they'd met, but it wasn't just about sex. It was much, much more. Her feelings for him proved that to her.

She was certain he felt the same way too.

She rolled over as quietly as she could, and sat on the side of the bed.

She should go. Missy would be worried – it was the middle of the night.

An arm reached out and grabbed her around the waist. His voice was husky. "Where are you off to in such a hurry?"

"I should go. Missy will be worried," she told him quietly.

He laughed. "Missy knows exactly where you are, and probably what we're doing," he said with a chuckle. "Might as well make the most of this comfy bed, eh?"

He pulled her back into the warm bed, and Grace curled herself up next to him. Right where she wanted to be.

* * *

The day had finally come.

The cottage was ready, and she could move in. Her new bed and bedding had been delivered, and three recliners were on the way.

She finally had her truck and horse trailer back, and she'd bought groceries and other basic supplies.

The cottage would soon feel like a real home, she had no doubt. Jordon was such a gem for letting her stay there.

She stood in the middle of the kitchen and took a deep breath. Was this really happening? As soon as she was properly settled, she was going to start working on her horse riding business.

It was an exciting time for her.

New home, new business. A whole new start in life. And love.

She sensed him before she saw him, and suddenly looked up, taken aback.

He was standing in the doorway, a smile on his face. "Well, hello, Grace," he said.

He was silhouetted by the sun, but she could see part of his face. He was wearing a sneer.

He wasn't a big man, quite scrawny in fact. Around 5'8" she guessed and had long straggly black hair. It was greasy and looked like it hadn't been washed in days.

A whiff of perspiration hit her nostrils, and she took a step backwards. She'd known he was around because of the distant sightings, but he'd never gotten this close before. It worried her.

"Get out. Now!" Grace yelled at him, pulling her phone out of her pocket. She hesitated. Who should she call? Jordon? Chase, Jordon's brother was the local Sheriff. Perhaps she should call him.

He just laughed at her. "Or you'll do what? Run to your boyfriend's brother?" He paused. For effect, Grace decided. *"The sheriff."*

So, he'd been watching her since she'd arrived. What would have happened if Jordon hadn't turned up when she'd put her truck down a ditch? Would he have cornered her then? It didn't bear thinking about.

When she heard a truck pull up outside, Grace let go of the breath she didn't realize she'd been holding. *Jordon.*

She looked up, and her stalker was gone.

* * *

Chase came to them.

He had his Sheriff's uniform on, along with his cowboy hat. Come to think of it, even at the house, Grace had never seen him without it.

His pen poised over his notepad, he began to question Grace. "How long has this man been stalking you?"

Grace looked to Jordon for support, and he held her hand. "A few years maybe." She tossed her long brown hair back over her shoulder, as though it meant nothing.

"A few years?" Chase said, his voice a little higher volume than usual.

Grace straightened her shoulders and glared at him. "Yes, a few damned years! What did you want me to do? No one took it seriously. Not the police, not my manager. No one!"

He looked at her in shock, then shook his head. "Sorry, that was way out of line."

"Yes, it was." Jordon came to her defense. "Grace is not the criminal here. A little respect, Bro."

She was shaking and was sure Jordon would feel it.

His voice was softer this time. Brotherly. "Of course, she's not." Chase turned to her. "Sorry Grace, just trying to get the info and catch the mongrel."

"Look," Grace said impatiently, staring into her lap. "Bottom line is I have no idea who that idiot is. He's been following me for as long as I can remember." Her lip quivered, but she was not going to let her emotions take over. "Until now, he's never come this close. I've only ever seen him in the distance, and he's even waved a time or two."

"Brazen," Chase said. And he didn't look happy about it.

She stared at Chase. "Do you think he's dangerous?" Her voice began to break, and Jordon squeezed her hand. "I mean, is it safe for me to stay at the cottage alone?"

Chase glanced at her, then his brother. He pushed his hat back on his head to reveal a little more of his forehead. "I really can't answer that for certain, but I'd suggest not." He stared at his brother, daring him to let her stay there alone.

Jordon stepped up to the plate. "No problem. I'll stay with her. Surely he will keep his distance if there's someone else around?"

"He didn't when Missy and I were out riding," Grace said in a rush, suddenly wishing she'd said nothing.

The two men looked at each other. Maybe it was more of a problem than they were letting on.

* * *

Grace went into town alone.

She still had a few supplies to get, and she wanted to check out the local boutique. Missy had told her River Valley had nearly everything she'd ever need, and Grace preferred to shop local, as her friend did.

She called into Aunt Lizzie's Kitchen and ordered a coffee and cake. It was nice to sit down and have a break.

"No Jordon today," Lizzie asked. Grace could see her interest was peaked.

Grace chuckled. "Uh uh. I'll be clothes shopping after I leave here. There is no way I'd want him hanging around!"

Lizzie laughed in agreement. The two women were definitely on the same page. "I love your establishment," Grace told her. "Café by day, restaurant by night. Do you ever have time off?"

"Not often, but I love being here," she answered. "And I do have staff that can run the

74

place without me." Grace could see the love on her face. This was obviously a labor of love.

The café was almost empty, which surprised Grace. She'd never seen it this empty before. Lizzie must have seen her looking around. "We have peaks and troughs," she said. "It's nice to slow down now and then." Lizzie sat down opposite Grace, taking her by surprise.

"I can see you have real feelings for our Jordon," Lizzie told her. "He's... he's somewhat fragile. I'm not going to delve into your private life, but wanted to ask you to be careful with him."

"Careful?" Grace was taken aback. "What do you mean by careful?"

Lizzie chose her words cautiously and reached out to cover Grace's hand with her own. "He was left at the altar, love." Lizzie stared directly into her eyes. "An hour before the wedding was to take place."

Grace gasped. She knew, but until now didn't realize how close this community really was. "I know," she told Lizzie. "I would never hurt Jordon. I love him."

The server came over and placed Grace's order in front of her.

"I really like you, Lizzie," Grace said. "And I love that you are looking out for Jordon. That makes you extra special in my book."

Lizzie squeezed her hand and smiled. "You're alright yourself," she said. "Enjoy your coffee and cake. I'm sure we'll see each other some other time." Before she could answer, Lizzie was gone.

Until she'd said the words out loud, Grace hadn't realized she had gone from infatuation to loving Jordon. But deep down she felt it had always been that way.

Did he love her back, she wondered?

* * *

Grace stopped in front of the little boutique Missy had raved over.

The clothes on the models were pretty, but not her style. Hopefully there was a bigger range inside. As she stepped away from the window, about to walk inside, she saw his silhouette in the glass.

She didn't turn around, just kept on walking into the store.

It wasn't very big inside, but there was a nice assortment. Clothes she could easily wear. She mostly wore jeans and western shirts, and there was certainly lots of those here.

But what she really wanted was more fancy clothes. Something to light up Jordon's face like the outfit she'd worn to Aunt Lizzies Kitchen on their date.

She found a rack with some pretty off-the-shoulder tops. The items in this store were top quality. Which was what she liked. She picked four different colors and styles and went to the changing rooms.

"Let me know if you need any assistance," the young girl told Grace.

As she tried on the items, she sensed him in the store. Then that putrid odor hit her. He was definitely here. Chase was right – he *was* brazen now.

She made her choices and returned to the counter with them. Glancing out the window, she spotted him across the road.

"I'll take these three," she said. "But I want to continue browsing for skirts, if that's okay."

The assistant put the tops aside, and showed her the new arrivals, some of which Grace loved.

She adored that style with the tiny pleats at the front. One of them also had inbuilt slash around the waist, which continued down the front for a bit.

She took five to try this time, as well as a couple of plainer skirts from another rack.

It was a hard decision, because she liked them all, but chose just three. She returned to the counter, and spotted him across the road, just as before.

"I'll take these three skirts as well," Grace said, pulling out her credit card. The assistant smiled. If she was on commission, it would be a good day for her.

She took her packages and left the store. It was getting late now, nearly time for the shops to close. The only thing left on her to-do list was a visit to the bakery, then she would go home and prepare dinner.

The bakery was only a few doors down, since the township of River Valley was so tiny, so she put her bags of clothes in her truck, then walked to the quaint little bakery.

Once her final purchases were made, Grace returned to her truck and left for home.

She took a deep breath. *She could do this. She would do this!*

* * *

By the time Grace returned to the cottage, it was beginning to get dark. Not pitch black, but more like twilight.

Now she was living there, she'd brought Spirit to his new home. She packed away all her shopping, then went to feed him out in the stables.

Thank goodness Jordon had the hindsight to add lighting out here when he'd had electricity installed to the cottage. It would be downright creepy otherwise.

Especially with her stalker hanging around.

After feeding Spirit and giving him a rubdown, she put his blanket on him, ready for sleep. He seemed to be enjoying his new abode, but she wondered if he was missing the other horses.

She would have to remedy that very soon.

As she returned to the cottage, Grace realized she hadn't locked the front door. It wasn't something she'd normally do after simply going to the stables, but with Mr Stinky hanging around, it would be an extra precaution she should probably take.

She shrugged it off. *Was he really so brazen as to enter the cottage while she was in the stables?* She didn't think so.

Grace decided to make dinner – chicken salad. She'd bought a cold chicken in town, and was making a tossed salad to go with it.

She poured herself a glass of wine, and set about preparing the salad. She'd bought some bowls and a dinner set yesterday. It was like totally starting over.

Back home in Wyoming, she had a fully furnished unit with everything included. She loved that little unit, but being on the circuit, she was rarely there. So she'd bit the bullet, and rented it out, opting to stay in motels instead.

Now she had to decide whether to sell her unit, or keep it as an investment. It would depend on how much she'd have to pay for the property she eventually purchased, if she went down that route.

This little cottage had really grown on her, but she would only stay if Jordon let her lease it, instead of staying rent free.

She was getting the salad dressing out of the refrigerator when she heard a sound behind her. for a moment, she stood glued to the spot.

She turned slowly.

"Hello Grace," Mr Stinky said confidently. "Have you made enough for me? I am invited, aren't I?" he said with a sneer on his face.

Grace held the dressing in her hand. She was shaking, but was determined not to let her guard down. "I saw you in town," she said, her voice a little shaky.

"Nice choice of clothing," he said matter-of-factly. "Maybe you could give me a show after we eat?"

He was so cocky it worried Grace. A lot.

"Or maybe she won't." It was Jordon's voice. Mr Stinky spun toward Jordon. Dismay on his face.

"She definitely won't," Chase added, coming up from behind him. He stepped forward and cuffed the intruder, who was not happy about being set up.

Two deputies were outside, and took him out to their truck, which was parked quite a distance away so as not to be seen or heard.

Chase had concocted a plan where Grace would spend the day in town alone. They all knew Mr Stinky wouldn't be able to resist watching her without worrying about being caught. What he didn't know was Grace had a tail the entire time. One of the deputies went in plain clothes, in an unmarked car.

She was never in danger.

Jordon went over to Grace and took her in his arms. "It's over," he whispered, then kissed her lightly on the forehead. "Have I told you how much I love you?" he said quietly.

"I love you too," she said. "I think I have since the moment we met."

He brushed away the tears that slowly slid down her face. After all these years, she finally felt completely safe. And loved.

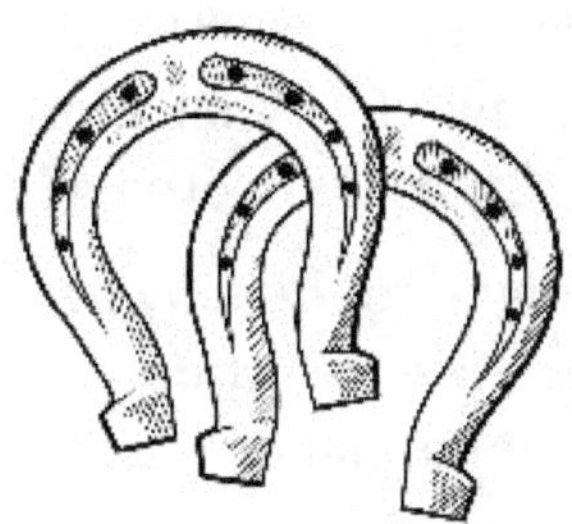

Chapter Five

After all the kerfuffle had settled, and Mr Stinky was gone, it had taken ages for Grace to feel her normal self again.

After finishing her wine, she was feeling a little better, but Jordon poured her another, despite her protests.

She was beginning to feel hungry, and finished making the salad, despite Jordon offering to do it for her.

They sat at the table, eating mostly in silence.

"Your brother is a miracle worker," Grace suddenly said out of the blue.

Jordon looked up in surprise. "Chase – a miracle worker? How so?"

"Easy," Grace told him. "I've lived with that mongrel in the background for years, and no one could do anything about it. Then along comes Chase, and it's all done and dusted. Just like that." She clicked her fingers.

"He is definitely good at his job. He's put his heart and soul into it since his wife died in a car accident some years ago."

Grace dropped her cutlery in shock. "His wife died? Oh my goodness, that's awful." What more did this family have to endure, Grace wondered.

"It's alright Grace. He might not be fully over it, but he is living his life the best he can." Jordon put his hand over hers and squeezed her hand.

"I have an apple pie in that ancient wood-fired stove," Grace said. "I have no idea how well it will turn out," she said, trying to change the subject.

Jordon sniffed the air. "Smells good."

He cleared their plates from the table, then opened the oven door. "Looks pretty darned good to me."

"I even have fresh cream!"

Jordon took the pie from the oven and cut it up. Missy had done a good job teaching Grace how to cook. He'd have to remember to thank her.

"This is incredible," he said, taking the last mouthful of his pie. "Are you nearly done? I have plans for supper." His eyes lit up, and Grace was ready to try out her brand-new king-sized bed with its fresh new bedding.

* * *

Grace couldn't believe her horse riding school was finally up and running, after all these months. She'd worked hard to get to this point, and Jordon had certainly helped her along.

Through his veterinarian work, he'd managed secure the horses she needed. Ten to begin with, and an option for more down the track.

It had been a long hard road, but would be worth it in the end, she was certain.

The stables had been extended to accommodate the additional horses, fresh hay – and plenty of it - had been delivered, and there was a sign out the front – *River Valley Horse Riding School*.

She'd even managed to get a stable hand. She only needed a skeleton staff now, but when her business was in full swing, she would need more stable hands.

She finally had everything she'd ever wanted; her own business, a place to call home, and most of all, her wonderful fiancée, Jordon.

As her soul-mate came up from behind and massaged her stiff shoulders, Grace groaned. She knew where she wanted to be; anywhere Jordon happened to be.

She'd made the move to Jordon's place some weeks ago, and the cottage had become nothing more than an office. She was not sorry for all the work she'd done on the cottage. Without it, they would never have found great grandmother Bessie's diary, which was turning out to be quite insightful.

And she would never have gotten as close to Jordon as she had.

Jordon still had plans for the old family cottage, and was determined to open his domestic animal veterinary clinic. It seemed a long way off right now, but Grace knew they would get there eventually.

* * *

Grace stepped out of the shower and wrapped a thick, fluffy towel around herself. She twisted her long brown hair into another towel and began to dry herself off.

She sat down and rubbed body cream all over herself. After all, today was special. It was the beginning of her new life.

She put on her underwear, then a light dressing gown, and began to dry off her hair. If she left it in the towel for too long, it would just be a tangled mess, and that just wouldn't do.

As she ran the brush through her long locks, she sat on the end of the bed contemplating the life changes she'd undergone since she arrived in River Valley less than a year ago.

That momentous night she'd met Jordon Callahan, the love of her life.

What would her life have been like if they hadn't crossed paths?

Grace took a deep breath. She didn't want to think about it.

With her hair now dry, she styled it into a French plait, adding three soft pink flowers intermittently. When she was done, she added some glitter gel, which made her hair sparkle.

She looked at herself in the full-length mirror. She was happy. She was truly happy – more than she'd been in many years. Why she had left it so long to visit River Valley, she'd never know.

This was where she needed to be, where she felt at home, where she felt more loved than she'd ever been in her life. River Valley was where her heart was, and always would be.

Grace picked up her makeup and began to apply a light covering of eye shadow. Blue to match her eyes. She'd never been one to wear much make up, and today would be no exception.

She added a little pink to her lips and put on her dangling earrings.

She opened the closet where her stunning chiffon dress hung. She fingered the soft material and watched the tiny glitter shine in the light.

Taking it off the hanger, she slid it over her head, and reached behind herself, and struggled to do up the zipper. *Where was Jordon when she needed him?*

Heart racing, she ran her hands down her knee length dress. The soft pink creation was an off the shoulder design and tapered in at the waistline. The matching silk ribbon at the bodice held a tiny pink flower – similar in color and design to the flowers she'd added to her hair.

From the waist it was pleated, giving the dress a fifties look.

Last of all, Grace added her sparkling pink shoes.

She was very nervous about tonight – their engagement party – and was sure Jordon would be too.

Grace checked herself over. Everything seemed to be fine. She was finally ready.

She heard a light tap on the door, and knew it would be her fiancée, Jordon. Neither of them really wanted a party, but Jordon's brothers insisted. After all, they'd said, it wasn't every day their little brother got engaged.

As she opened the door, Grace was breathless. Jordon was dressed all in white. His perfectly tailored suit was white, as was his shirt and silk tie. He even had a small white corsage attached to his lapel.

"Ready?" he asked, as he entered.

Grace stood staring. He was certainly a sight to behold. "As I'll ever be."

She grabbed her clutch, and they walked to Jordon's truck, ready for the trip to Rory and Missy's place, and their engagement party.

* * *

Lizzie had been asked to cater for the party, which, as it turned out, would be one of the biggest events in River Valley that year.

There were loads of hot foods; a variety of roast meats, assorted roast vegetables, fried rice, gravy, and apple sauce. There were mini pies and sausage rolls, mini quiches, as well as lots of other finger foods.

Lizzie provided a huge assortment of desserts, including cakes, muffins, apple pies, cherry pies, and more.

Missy and Rory had hired a marquee, and tables were set out for the guests.

The party was in full swing by the time they arrived, and Missy looked rather nervous. Grace wondered if she thought they'd ditched on her, opting to stay away.

She would never do that to her best friend.

The pair mingled with crowd, which consisted of family and friends from River Valley, as well as other places.

After an hour or so, Rory called for quiet.

"Thanks everyone for coming tonight," he said, his cowboy hat firmly on his head. "We are so pleased to have you all here to celebrate my little brother's engagement."

Jordon rolled his eyes.

"Oh, and Grace's too, of course!" He shook his brother's hand, and hugged Grace. "Okay, little bro, time for you to make a speech," he told Jordon.

Jordon took the floor. "We'd like to thank everyone for coming tonight," he said. "We are genuinely pleased that you were able to make it." He looked across at Grace, and she nodded.

"We have a little surprise for you all," he told the throng.

Grace heard the gasp of the crowd, no doubt wondering what they were up to.

"I would like to introduce you to Andrea Cummins," he indicated to a woman standing quietly in the corner. "Our wedding celebrant!"

As everyone began to talk between themselves, Rory rushed up to his brother and gave him a man-hug.

Missy was right behind him. As she hugged Grace, she whispered in her ear. "I told you your secret would be safe with me. Now we'll be more than best friends, we'll be sisters," she said, tears in her eyes.

The End

Enjoy this story?

Check out the Callahan Brothers great-great grandmother Bessie's story:

<u>Bessie – The Soiled Doves Series</u>

https://www.amazon.com/Bessie-Soiled-Doves-Book-8-ebook/dp/B077BZQZXT/

<u>For a full list of the Callahan Brothers Series</u>

https://www.amazon.com/gp/product/B078W9YCP5?ref=series_rw_dp_labf

About the Author

Multi-published, award-winning author, Cheryl Wright, former secretary, debt collector, account manager, writing coach, and shopping tour hostess, loves reading.

She writes romantic suspense, contemporary romance, and western romance.

She lives in Melbourne, Australia, and is married with two adult children and has six grandchildren.

When she's not writing, she can be found in her craft room making greeting cards, or in her kitchen baking.

Check out <u>Cheryl's Amazon page</u> –

https://www.amazon.com/author/cherylwright

for a full list of her other books.

Other Links:

http://cheryl-wright.com

https://www.facebook.com/cherylwrightauthor

<u>Join my newsletter</u>

http://cheryl-wright.com/newsletter.html

9 780097 567295 2